LITTLE DOG LOST, LITTLE DOG FOUND

By ESPHYR SLOBODKINA

Jet was a cute little puppy that Johnny loved and played with. The day the dog catcher took him to the animal shelter, Johnny looked all over for him, but couldn't find him. A lonely lady did find him, though, but what happened to Johnny? Look at the pictures and see how it turned out.

❊ ❊

Dewey Decimal Classification: E

little dog Lost,

Story and Pictures by
ESPHYR SLOBODKINA

little dog Found

Found

CADMUS BOOKS

1961 First Cadmus Edition

THIS SPECIAL EDITION IS PUBLISHED BY ARRANGEMENT WITH
THE PUBLISHERS OF THE REGULAR EDITION
ABELARD-SCHUMAN LIMITED
BY
E. M. HALE AND COMPANY
EAU CLAIRE, WISCONSIN

Johnny had a little dog.

He was very black
and he was very fast.
So Johnny called him

JET.

Jet was a good little dog.
He found the ball
when Johnny lost it
and brought it back.

He watched over
Johnny's things.

And he never, never
chased stray cats!

But Jet had one very bad habit!
Jet was careless, and no matter
how Johnny tried to teach him
to be more careful, he always
managed to lose his dog-tag. . . .

One day it happened!

The Dog Catcher came and saw
that Jet had no dog-tag.

He caught him in his net

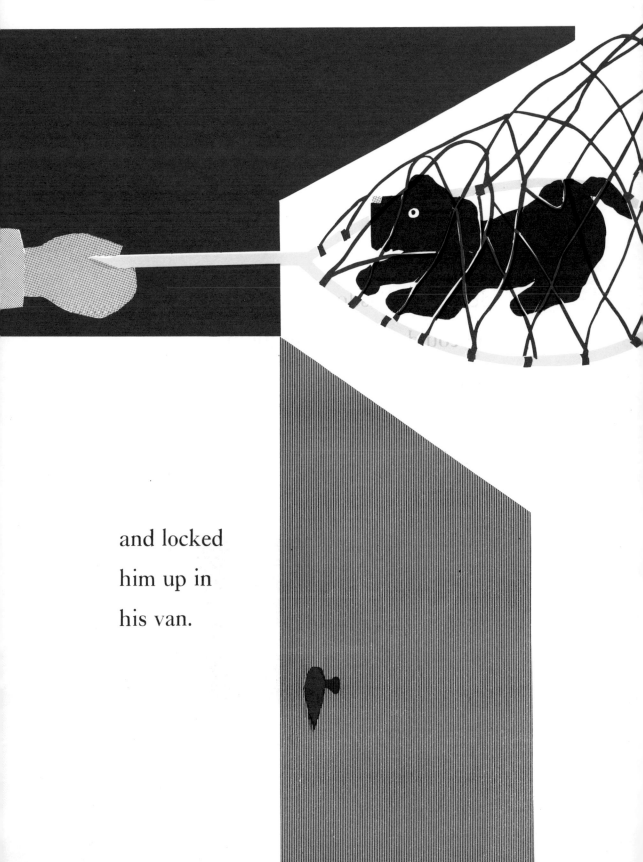

and locked
him up in
his van.

Jet barked as loudly as
he could and tried to jump
out of the window.

CITY ANIMAL SHELTER

But the Dog Catcher only
pulled down the dark
window shade,

got into the driver's seat,

and drove off.

CITY ANIMAL SHELTER

Johnny looked for Jet everywhere:
He went to the Big Policeman,
but the Policeman
had not seen Jet.

He went to the Dog Catcher,
but the Dog Catcher
did not remember Jet.

He went everywhere and asked
everybody,

but

nobody knew anything
about Jet.

JET WAS LOST!

Johnny was very sad and lonely
because he could not find Jet.

He stayed in his room most of the time
and looked out of the window,
hoping that Jet would come back.

At the same time,

a lady named Miss Julia Jones

sat at her window, feeling very lonely too.

She sighed and said:

"What I need is a little dog

to keep me company."

So, Miss Julia Jones got up,
put on her fine hat and coat,

got into her big car,
and asked the chauffeur
to drive her to the
City Animal Shelter.

Miss Jones looked at a lot of little dogs.

She looked at skinny ones and
                    chubby ones.

She looked at sleek ones and
                    fluffy ones.

She looked at red ones
and at white ones.

She liked them all.

But the one she liked the best was
a friendly little,
quick little

JET-BLACK
DOG.

And so Jet
(for, of course,
it was Jet!)

went to live with
Miss Jones to keep
her company.

He was
washed,

and
he was
clipped;

and he got a new
bright-yellow leash.

He was also taught to heel,

and to sit,
and to lie down,
and to beg for
sugar . . .

and he
learned many other tricks
a well-bred little dog
should know.

Jet had no trouble learning
all these things;
Jet was very
clever.

But he felt
sad and lonely, because:

there was no ball to find;
there were no things to watch;
there were no cats *not* to chase;
and, worst of all, there was
no Johnny!

One day when Jet and
the chauffeur were
walking slowly
down the block,

a ball rolled past them, and off
the sidewalk.

Jet jumped after the ball
and brought it back
to the waiting children.

They crowded around him
and shouted:

"It's Jet! It's Jet!
JET IS FOUND!"

And so he was.

But what about Miss Julia Jones?

Well, when Miss Jones
found out that Jet
was really Johnny's
little dog, she let
Johnny keep Jet
    (with his bright-yellow leash
    and the new dog-tag that
    could never be lost),

because she was a kind lady.

And, besides,

she was not lonely any more because

Johnny and Jet and all the
other children and their pets

became her very good friends!